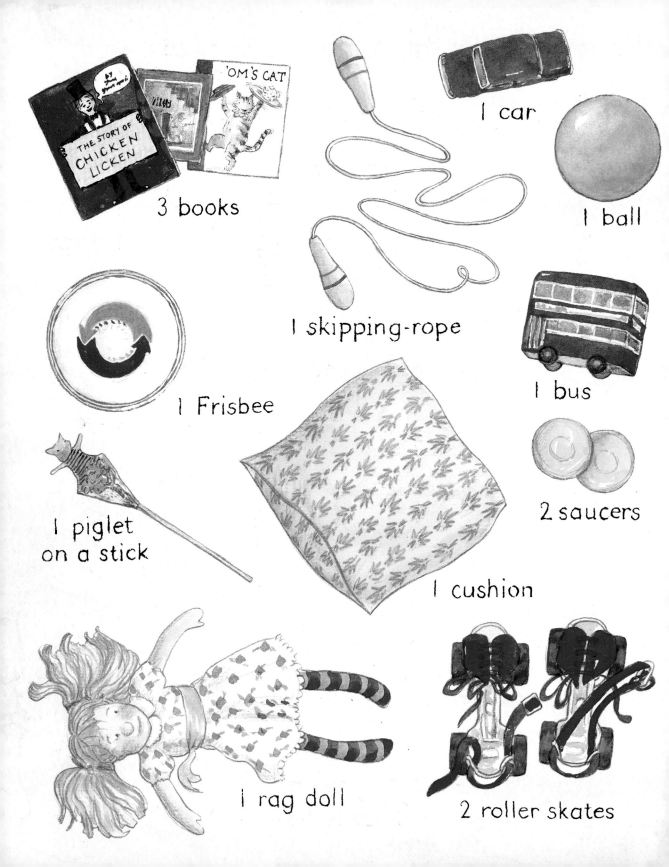

3 books

1 car

1 ball

1 skipping-rope

1 Frisbee

1 bus

2 saucers

1 piglet on a stick

1 cushion

1 rag doll

2 roller skates

2 bricks

1 ruler

1 dress

1 rabbit

1 telephone

1 yo-yo

2 cups

1 jigsaw puzzle

1 quilt

1 teddy bear

1 teapot

For Leanne and Nathan

First published 1987 by
Walker Books Ltd
87 Vauxhall Walk
London SE11 5HJ

This edition published 1989
Reprinted 1991, 1992, 1993, 1994

© 1987 Penny Dale

Printed and bound in Hong Kong by
Sheck Wah Tong Printing Press Ltd

British Library Cataloguing in Publication Data
A catalogue record for this book is
available from the British Library.
ISBN 0-7445-1225-5

Bet you can't!

WRITTEN AND ILLUSTRATED BY
Penny Dale

WALKER BOOKS
LONDON

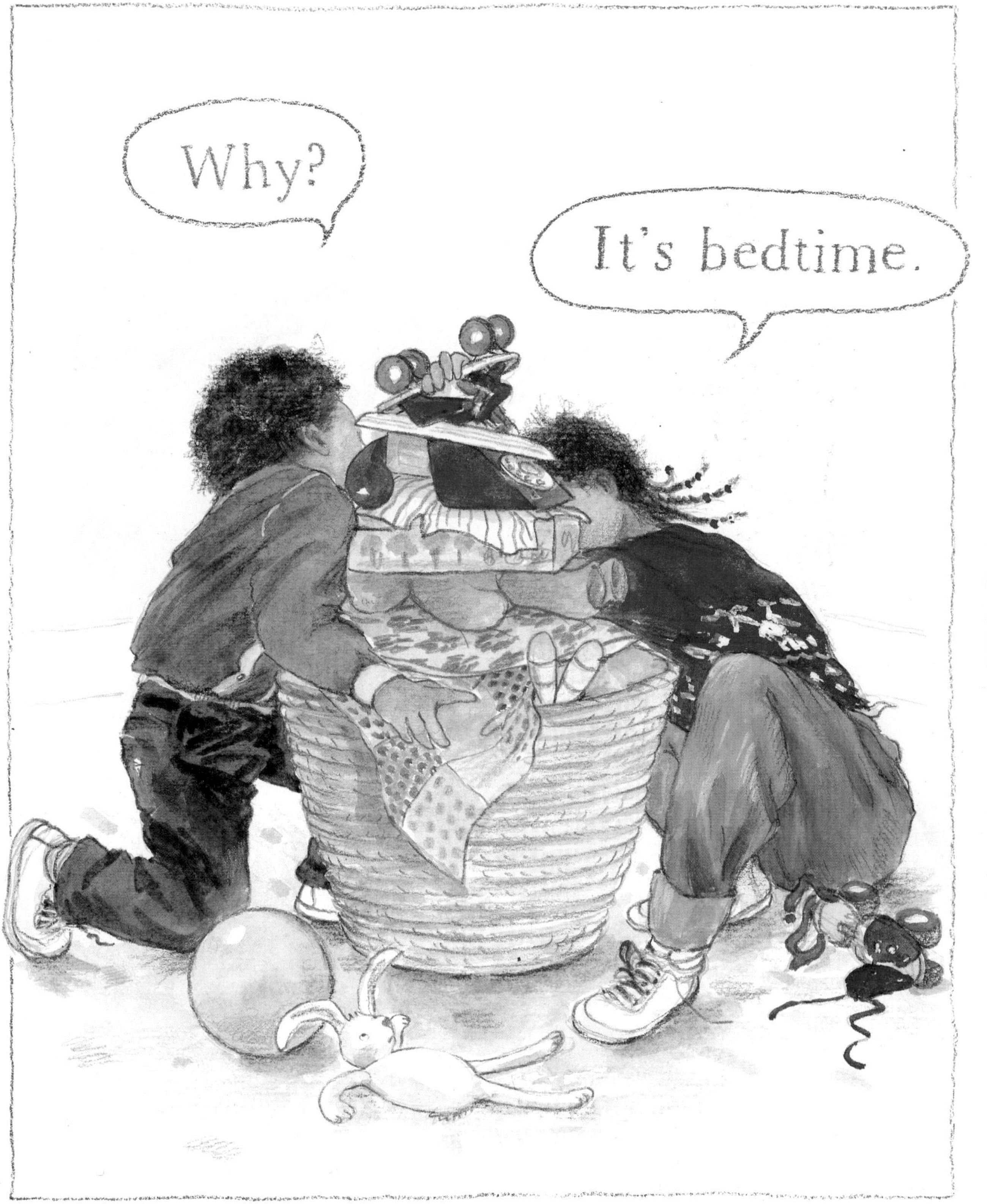
Why?
It's bedtime.

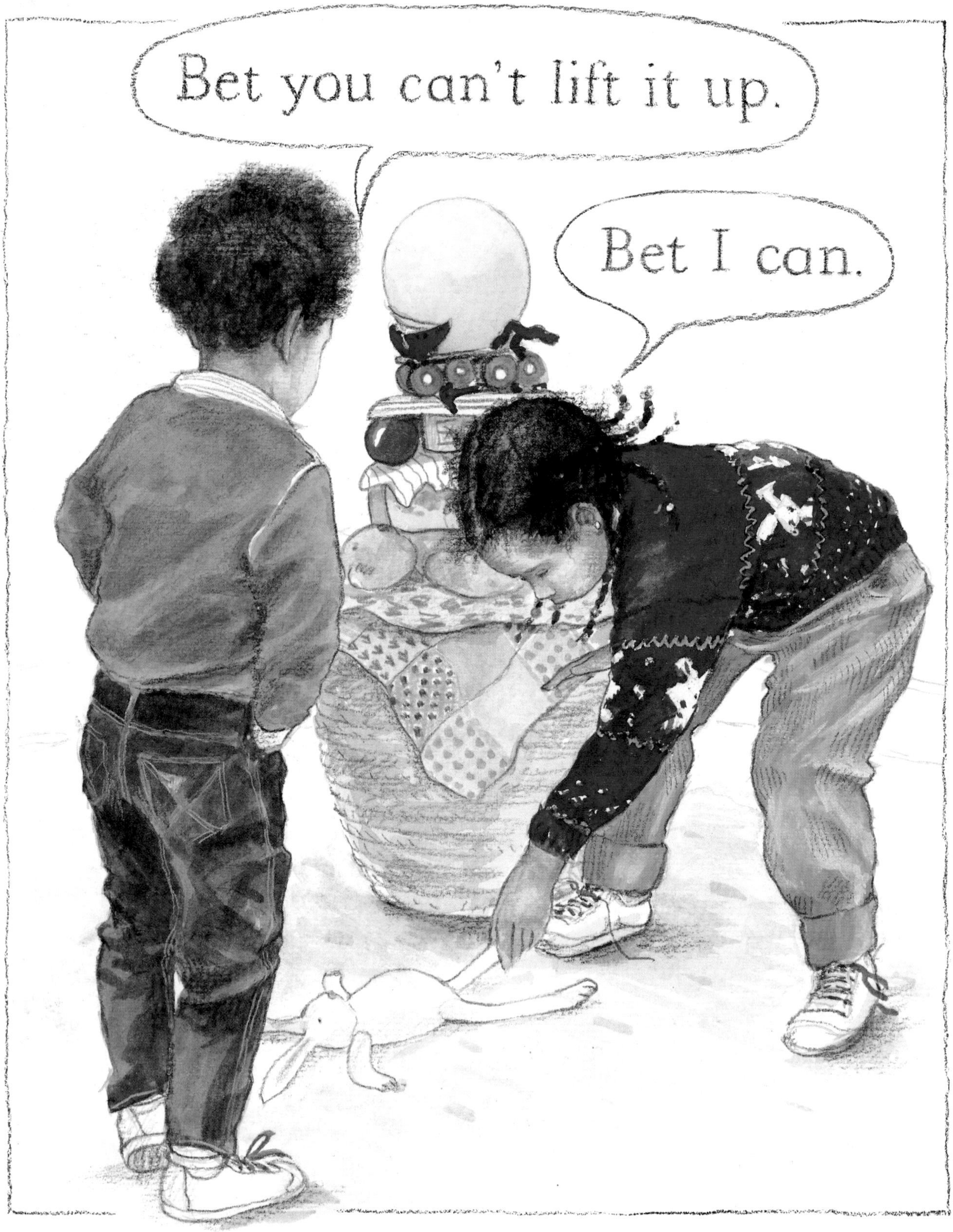
Bet you can't lift it up.
Bet I can.

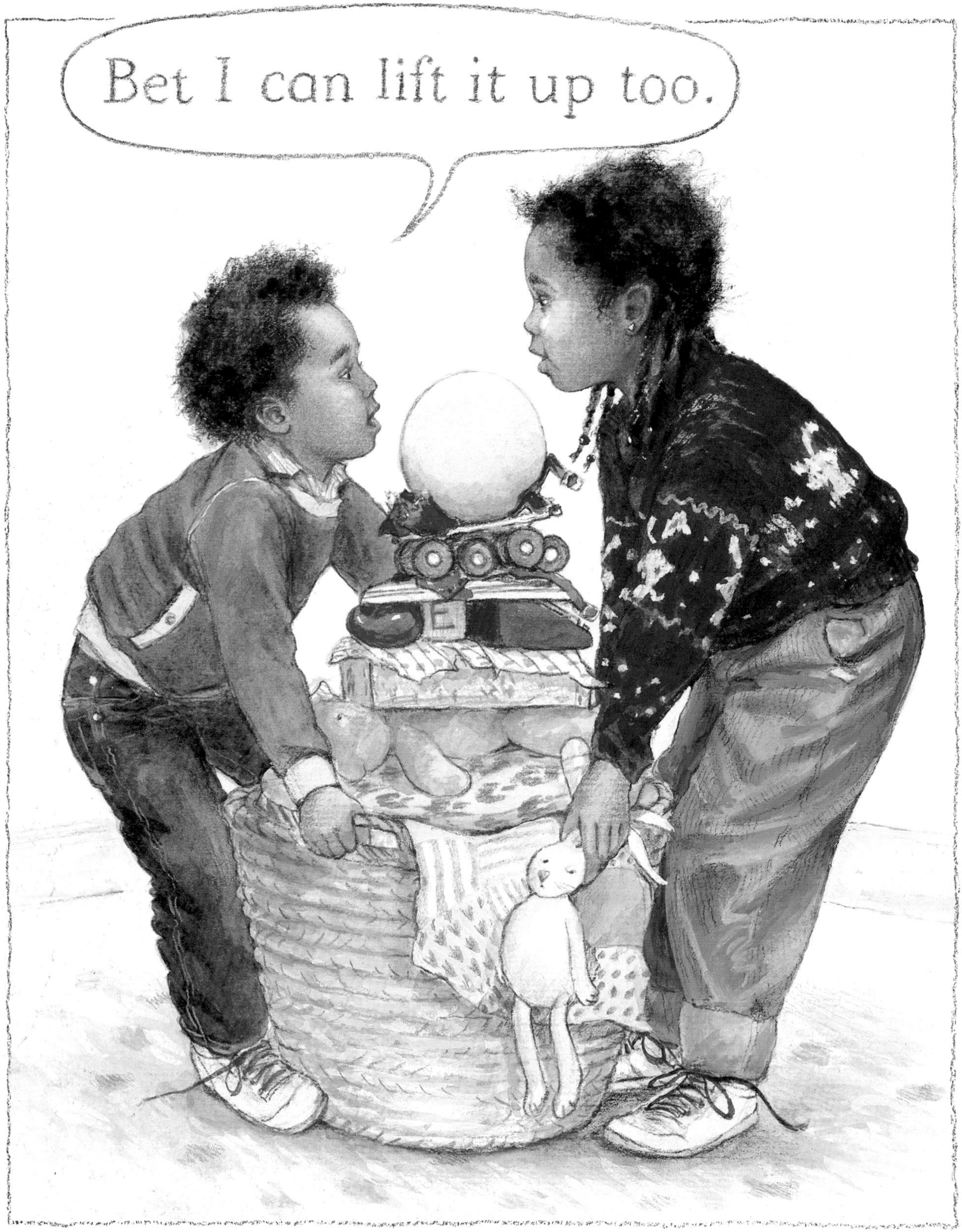
Bet I can lift it up too.

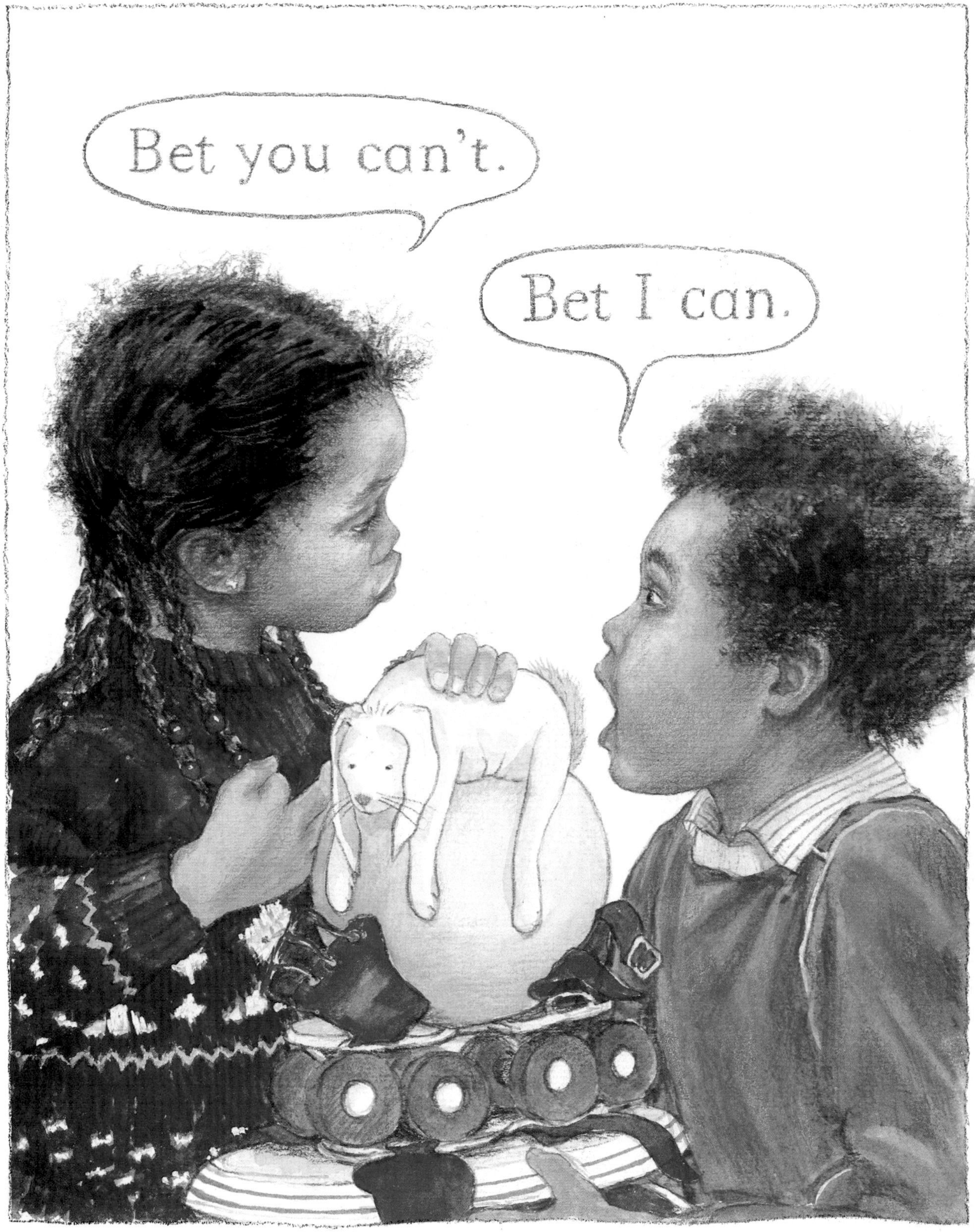
Bet you can't.
Bet I can.

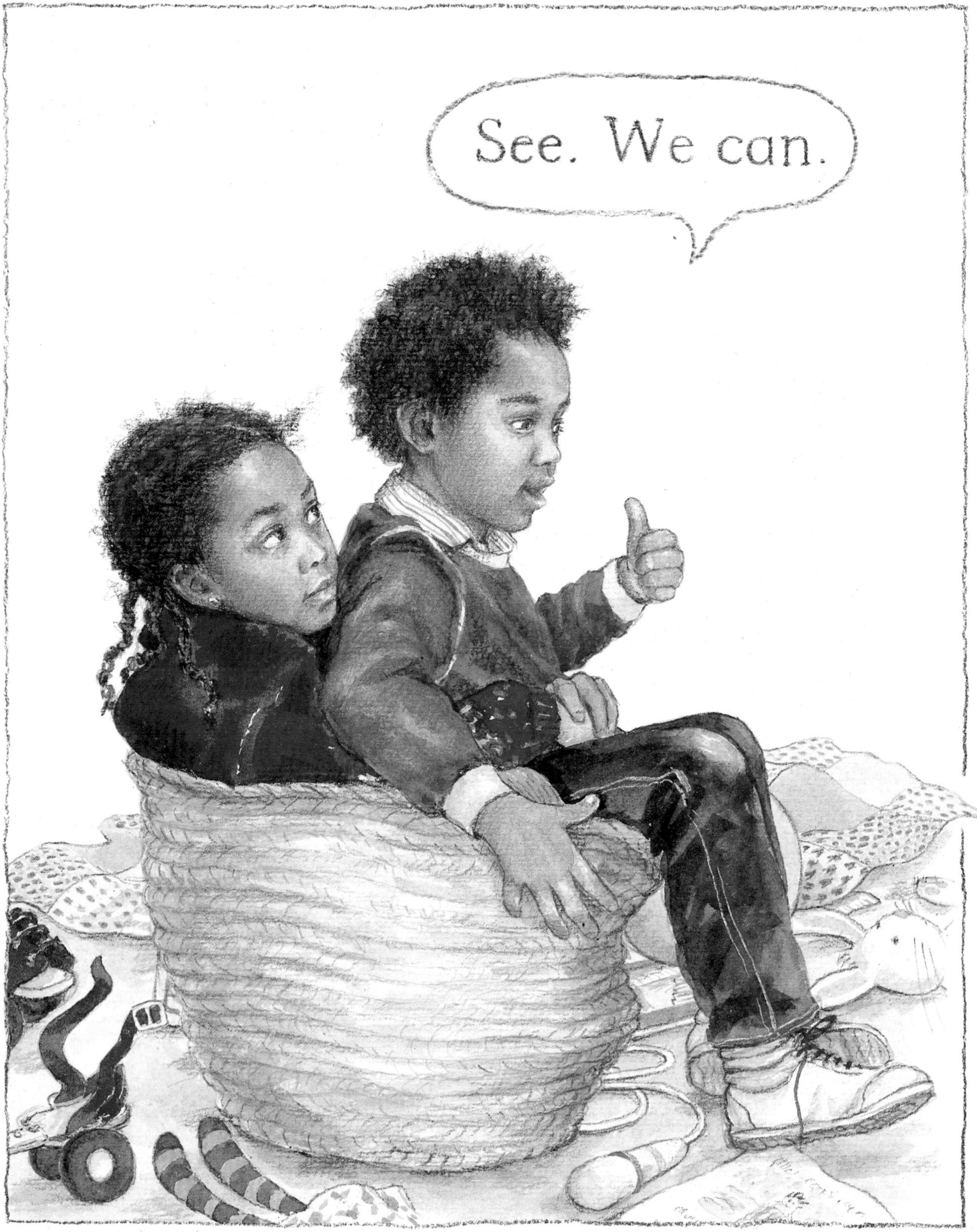
See. We can.

3 books

1 car

1 skipping-rope

1 ball

1 Frisbee

1 bus

2 saucers

1 piglet
on a stick

1 cushion

1 rag doll

2 roller skates

2 bricks

1 ruler

1 dress

1 telephone

1 yo-yo

1 rabbit

2 cups

1 jigsaw puzzle

1 quilt

1 teddy bear

1 teapot

MORE WALKER PAPERBACKS
For You to Enjoy

Also by Penny Dale

WAKE UP, MR. B!

"Perceptive, domestic illustrations fill a varied cartoon-strip format …
making this a lovely tell-it-yourself picture book."
The Good Book Guide
ISBN 0-7445-1467-3   £3.99

TEN IN THE BED

"A subtle variation on the traditional nursery song, illustrated with wonderfully
warm pictures … crammed with amusing details."
Practical Parenting
ISBN 0-7445-1340-5   £3.99

THE STOPWATCH
written by David Lloyd

When Gran gives Tom a stopwatch, he times everything – from how fast
he can eat his food to how long he can stand on his head!

"The illustrations are wonderful… A good early reader."
BBC Radio
ISBN 0-7445-1358-8   £2.99

**Walker Paperbacks are available from most booksellers, or by post from
Walker Books Ltd, PO Box 11, Falmouth, Cornwall TR10 9EN.**

To order, send: title, author, ISBN number and price for each book ordered, your full name and address
and a cheque or postal order for the total amount, plus postage and packing:

UK and BFPO Customers – £1.00 for first book, plus 50p for the second book and plus 30p for each additional book to a maximum charge of £3.00.
Customers – £2.00 for first book, plus £1.00 for the second book and plus 50p per copy for each additional book.
are correct at time of going to press, but are subject to change without notice.